MW00938248

Jaxon's Magical Adventure with Black Inventors and Scientists

Tamara Shiloh

Illustrations by
Jo Ann Kairys

Just Imagine Books & Services
Richmond, California

Just Imagine...What If There Were No Black People in the World?
Book one: *Jaxon's Magical Adventure with Black Inventors and Scientists*
by Tamara Shiloh

Copyright © 2017 Just Imagine Books & Services

Published by
Just Imagine Books & Services

Books may be purchased by contacting the publisher and author at:
www.justimaginebooksandservices.com

ISBN: 978-0-9989696-0-2 (softcover)
ISBN: 978-0-9989696-1-9 (e-book)

LCCN: 2017912041

Publisher: Just Imagine Books & Services
Cover Design: Monica Thomas, TLC Graphics
Interior Layout: Nick Zelinger, NZ Graphics
Editor: Karin Fisher-Golton

Illustrations are courtesy of image public domains and the U.S. Patent office
Dr. Mark Dean permission granted by Dr. Mark Dean
Madame C. J. Walker permission granted by A'Lelia Bundles
Lewis Latimer permission granted by Queens Library

First Edition

Printed in the United States of America

Contents

1

A Frightening Idea

JAXON IS TIRED and not tired all at the same time. His mind is racing. He doesn't have any idea how he will ever get to sleep tonight. He's juiced because he's playing Dr. Martin Luther King, Jr. in the fourth-grade play, in celebration of Dr. King's birthday next week. He and his classmates rehearsed all afternoon and Jaxon, now more than ever, admires and respects Dr. King. He wants to do a super job so everyone will know what a good and important man Dr. King was.

He's pretty sure he was picked to play Dr. King because his and Dr. King's birthdays are on the same day and because he's the tallest boy in the class. This is all good, but he doesn't do well in front of an audience or when talking to strangers. He gets really nervous and stutters sometimes. He's gotta figure out how to overcome this before the play next week.

Jaxon is lying in bed thinking about all of this when suddenly, out of nowhere, this thought pops into his head *What if there were no Black people in the world?* He's not sure why he's thinking it, but it makes his head spin.

Okay! Calm down, he tells himself. His heart feels like it's beating out of his chest! Without thinking, he stands up and starts jumping up and down on his bed, blown away at the very thought of no Black people in the world! Worried and confused, he calls for his mom, forgetting that jumping on the bed is a real no-no.

In just a few seconds, his sister appears in his doorway, a little out of breath. "Jax, what the heck! You know you're not supposed

to jump on your bed. Get down before you fall and bust your head. Are you serious? Mom would lose it if she saw you jumping on the bed. So what's up?"

Jaxon stops jumping and plops down, breathing heavily. "I just had this weird thought and had to tell someone right away."

"Well, what is it crazy little boy?"

"Raimy, what if there were no Black people in the world? There would be no Dr. Martin Luther King! Whoa! There would be no me or you or Mom or Dad. Or...any other Black person! Man...I...I want to stop thinking about it because it's way too scary."

"Okay, calm down, Jax. Wow, that's a big worry for a cheery little fella like you. But you won't only have that to worry about if Mom catches you jumping on the bed," she warns.

Jaxon gives his sister that *I know* look.

"I couldn't relax, so I just had to start jumping on the bed."

"Uh huh. You had to? Seriously? Look little brother, there are other ways to calm down besides busting up your bed, like breathing. So breathe, okay? Deep breaths."

Jaxon takes a deep breath and sits down. It really does help him calm down. Taking breaths is supposed to help him stop stuttering too. He's really gotta remember that.

Raimy walks over to the bed and says, "Listen, with everything going on in the world, there have been times when that very question has popped into my head. I've thought about how different things would be."

"Yeah, huh," he replies softly as he climbs under his bedspread. He straightens his pajamas and stares at the sky blue ceiling with all the shiny stars, the spaceships, satellites, and rockets hanging down. "It was just weird how I couldn't stop thinking about Dr. King. And then I started thinking about the other people we discuss every year during Martin Luther King's birthday time and

Black History month. I was thinking, we study about the same people and what they did every year. And then the thought of no Black people in the world popped into my head."

His sister rubs his forehead.

"Raimy, just imagine…"

Raimy gasps and her eyes get big. She quickly puts her hand over his mouth so that he can't finish the sentence.

Jaxon's pushing his sister's hand from his mouth when his mom and dad stick their heads in the door.

His mom says, "We're back. Is everything okay?"

Raimy quickly removes her hand from Jaxon's mouth and answers, "Yep, we're fine Mom. I was just telling him goodnight," Raimy says smiling.

Jaxon, looking at Raimy, says, "Yeah Mom, I'm good."

Smiling, his dad says, "Hey, fella, don't forget we're going to the park tomorrow for our Saturday baseball. I have a short meeting at the office in the morning, but when I get home, we can go hit a few."

"I didn't forget," Jaxon assures him. He loves playing ball with his dad.

His dad steps over to the bed and gives Jaxon a high five and a hug. His mom kisses him on the forehead.

"Good night, Dad. Good night, Mom."

"Good night," they say back to him at the same time.

Raimy gets up and leaves the room right behind their parents and closes the door.

Jaxon can hear them talking to each other as they head downstairs.

The room gets dark for a second after Raimy closes the door. Then the stars on the ceiling light up and his little soldier night-light turns on automatically.

"Good night, Gran," he whispers under the stars, holding onto the necklace she gave him just before she passed away a year ago, right after his sister turned sixteen.

Jaxon always says goodnight to his grandmother. He misses her a lot. But he has the pretty shiny blue necklace to remind him of her.

2

Magic Words

OH MAN, JAXON still can't seem to get to sleep. He still has all these crazy thoughts running through his head about no Black people. He can't even imagine what that would be like, but it feels like it wouldn't be good at all.

As he's tossing and turning, his sister returns to his room and closes the door behind her. She sits down on his bed.

Jaxon sits straight up. "What's up Raimy? Why did you put your hand over my mouth? I was only going to say, 'Just imagine, what if there were no Black people in the world?'"

Raimy's mouth drops open, and her eyes get big. "Oh boy, Jax," she says. She gets up, paces around, then sits down again.

"I think it's time you learn something about the necklace Gran gave you. I know this is going to sound crazy, but that necklace has magical powers. You just have to say the words, 'just imagine,' followed by whatever it is you want."

Jaxon looks at his sister, his eyes blinking really fast. *Did she say "magic"??!! And whatever I want? No way!*

He catches his breath. "Powers? Don't be dumb. There's no such thing as magic."

"Yeah, I used to think the same thing. I had the same reaction that you're having right now," she said tapping him on his forehead.

He pulls out the necklace and stares at it. Something about the necklace makes him think there's a tiny possibility that this crazy idea could be true.

"Jax, something's different about what you wished for. I'm not really sure how what you asked for is going to happen. You see, somebody usually shows up to give you a hand with your wish. Kinda like the genie story, but not."

"What do you mean what I wished for? I didn't wish for anything. What are you talking about?"

"Yes, you did. You said, 'What if there were no Black people in the world?' after the magic words 'just imagine.' That's how you do the magic."

Jaxon's head starts to race even faster. "Whoa, so wh-wh-what's going to happen? Raimy are you sure about this?"

"That's what I'm wondering. See, I always wished for a specific thing to happen, but you didn't. Dude, I'm not sure how your wish is going to play out. Nothing happened, and something should have happened, I think," she says looking a little concerned.

"How do you know this? Did you have the necklace too? What do you mean something should have happened? Should I be scared? What did you wish for?"

"Okay, slow down little boy. Slow down. Yes, I did have the necklace when I was younger, about your age. But here's the deal—the magic only works three times a month and only until you're sixteen. And you don't need to know what I wished for. And, oh yeah, you should always save the third wish for just in case you need to undo a wish that goes wrong or something bad happens."

"What do you mean if s-s-something goes wrong?" he asks really wound up now.

"Hey little fella," she says putting a hand on his shoulder. "It's really going to be okay. Great even. You know what, I'll let Mom explain how all this works. I think she was going to wait until after your birthday to tell you stuff. I'll talk to Mom in the morning. She and Dad have already gone to bed. And since nothing happened, it can probably wait."

"Ah man, Raimy—this is sooooo cool! But only three times in a month!"

"Oh good, happy Jax is back. So yeah, Mom says it's called a lunar cycle. It's like from the first of the month to the end of the month. She can explain it better."

"Why only until I'm sixteen? Then what happens? Do I turn into something? Come on, Raimy. Tell me, please."

"Hold up! I know, Jax. I know you have a ton of questions. Believe me, I tried and tried to get Mom and Gran to answer those same questions. They answered some, but some I think they just didn't know. All I know is that I had to give the necklace back to Gran when I turned sixteen. Mom said the oldest person alive in the family, who had the necklace, has to give it to the next person to receive it, and that was you.

"And like I said, they were going to wait until you turn ten to tell you. Unfortunately, Gran passed away, and before Mom could tell you next week on your birthday, you, for some strange reason, said the magic words. That was freaky how you just said the words without even knowing what they meant.

"Jax, another thing I can tell you is that when you say the words, 'just imagine,' things and places might look different. You may even see things that you won't be able to explain. And someone will show up to help you out or explain things.

"Maybe someday we'll understand the hows and the whys of this power, but for now, you'll just have to go with the flow," she says with a simple smile.

"Who do I even ask? What about Dad? Can he answer these questions?"

"No, Dad didn't get the necklace and the magic. He knows about it, but that's about it. I'll let Mom explain that too. Don't worry, you'll kinda figure things out as you go."

"Well, if I find out anything, I'll let you know." He holds up his hand for a high five. She high fives him back.

Raimy stands and stares at him with a very serious look.

"Look Jax, I know this is hard to understand, but tomorrow you will have the power and the magic that comes with it. You probably have it now, but I don't understand what's really going on with your wish.

"And listen, you can say those words, but you really need to understand that you have to be careful and mindful when you are using the magic. Always save the third wish, just in case, and never, ever take off the necklace."

"I never have. Not since Gran gave it to me. I never will. Never." He pulls the necklace with the shiny blue pendant, out of his pajama top and shows it to Raimy.

She kisses him on the forehead. "Good night, Jax. We'll talk more tomorrow."

"Good night."

After Raimy leaves the room, Jaxon lays back down, stunned by what he just learned.

Sleep! No way will I ever be able to sleep again! What's gonna happen tomorrow? Ah man...

But before he knows it, Jaxon is nodding off. It has been a big, fantastic day.

Just as he's falling asleep, he thinks he hears his Gran whisper in his ear, "Sweet dreams, Baby."

3

A New Day

JAXON WAKES UP, a bit groggy, thinking, *Magic powers? Did Raimy actually say magic powers? She definitely said magic stuff will happen today. One thing I know is gonna happen is I get to play ball with my dad and hopefully go for ice cream or a movie afterward.*

He stretches, jumps out of bed, and immediately notices a few things are missing. His laptop for one. It was sitting on the table next to his bed. He wonders, *Did Raimy borrow it? No, she would have said something.*

What else is missing? The pencil sharpener is not sitting on the desk next to the pencil and my journal. And where are my tennis shoes?

He looks in his closet and not only are his tennis shoes missing, all of his shoes are gone!

He pulls out the necklace to make sure it's still there. Then he thinks, *Really, this is what I get? Hey, will I get my stuff back?*

Freaked out, Jaxon runs down the stairs, two at a time. When he gets to the bottom of the stairs, he scans the living room to see if anything is missing. The lamps are missing and his Gran's phone is gone.

"Raimy! Raimy!" he shouts running back to the stairs. He looks upstairs towards his sister's room.

"Come here! Please, Raimy. Come downstairs."

His sister walks down the stairs with that *see I toldja* look, amused and controlling a laugh.

"What's the matter, Jax? Why are you so excited?" She gives him a sneaky-looking smirk.

Jaxon paces back and forth at the bottom of the stairs. He crosses his arms over his head. "Look Raimy, the lamps and Gran's phone are missing. And some stuff in my room is missing too."

"Okay, Okay. Jax, relax. Stop pacing. Be still." She starts walking down the stairs and looks at him. "Well," she says, with a sparkle in her eyes, "now you have a good idea of how the powers of the necklace work."

He starts pacing again in front of the staircase. "Powers?" Okay, but...wow! I totally didn't expect this. Why are things missing?"

"It must have to do with the magic. Remember your question, 'what if there were no Black people?' Well, here's your answer. I think you're getting a taste of what it would be like. Look over there." She holds her hand up and points to where the lamps were and where the telephone was sitting.

"Now I get it!" she says excitedly. "You're gonna find out about the things Black people did that touch our lives. This," still gesturing at where the lamp and phone are missing, "is what happened because of what you wished for after saying 'just imagine.'"

"Are you kidding? No way! Really?" Jaxon stops pacing, but keeps looking around the house. His heart is beating a bit faster.

Looking at him sternly, his sister warns him, "This is no joke, Jaxon." He knows she's serious because she used his full name. "Even though you can have a lot of fun with your new power, you still need to remember to be very careful and not to make a wish that could put yourself or anyone else in danger."

She moves closer to him, "Jaxon, don't even think about testing this. I know you. Listen, if you wish for the wrong thing, it could backfire on you. Don't go saying or wishing for something crazy. And you know what crazy is. Just be smart about whatever you wish for. And remember, you already used one wish. Like I said last night, if you want to put things back the way they were, that's considered a wish too. So in a way, you only get two wishes. Mom can explain that as well."

"Ah man, this is w-w-way more than anything I could have imagined. This is like, like…unbelievable. I dunno, Black people must have invented a lot of stuff and some of the stuff that's in this house."

"Yep. Things are just getting wound up for you, little brother," she says, walking back up the stairs. "So have some fun and enjoy your day. It's probably going to be an interesting one. And, remember, behave yourself." She winks before rounding the corner.

"Behave?! I can have anything I want!" he mumbles quietly, grinning. *Let the fun begin*, he thinks, but he honestly doesn't really know what to do.

4

Magic in the Kitchen

JAXON IS STILL standing at the bottom of the stairs, staring at the living room. *Okay, now what?* He doesn't know whether to be excited or scared.

Heck, he thinks, *if Gran gave me this magic necklace, then she'll be there to help me if I get in trouble.* "Right Gran?" he asks in a whisper. He looks around half expecting her to answer him. Jaxon remembers to take a breath to calm down. He smiles thinking about his grandmother.

"This is all fine and dandy, but I'm thirsty as heck, hungry too."

He turns, walks into the kitchen to get a glass of orange juice and a bowl of cereal, and stops dead in his tracks.

The curtains are missing and other stuff, too. And there's a weird looking refrigerator in there. Like super old.

He goes to the counter, grabs a glass, and pours some of the orange juice someone left on the counter. He picks up the glass

Refrigerator
John Stanard

and walks over to take a closer look at the funky-looking refrigerator.

"What kind of refrigerator is this?" he says out loud to no one in particular.

A raspy voice fills the kitchen. "Without me there might not be no modern refrigerator."

Jaxon jumps back and drops the glass. It shatters, and he almost falls. He squeezes his eyes shut and opens them again. "Wh-wh-who are you?" he asks.

"My name is John Stanard. I'm the guy who invented a refrigerator with two doors," a man dressed in a brown striped suit and a white shirt, answers proudly. "I thought it would be a good idea if refrigerators had two compartments—one to keep the food cold and another one to keep the water and drinks cold. So when you want a drink, the food isn't exposed to warm air. Today you have the two-door refrigerator-freezer."

"I c-c-can see you." Jaxon steps back a little more to get some distance from this stranger.

"Yes. I can see you too," the man replies laughing.

"So th-th-this is about seeing and t-t-talking with the Black people who invented stuff? Will other people sh-sh-show up like you?"

"Yep, I'm pretty sure you'll see others today."

Jaxon is about to ask a question about the funny-looking refrigerator when he notices the dust pan and mop are missing. He hears voices behind him. He turns around and sees two men talking in the corner of the kitchen.

"Wh-wh-who are you?" he asks.

The taller of the two men speaks with a husky voice, "I'm Lloyd Ray. I invented an easy-to-use dust pan. Why was it easy to use, you might ask? Well, because my dust pan has a long handle so you don't have to bend down and get your hands dirty. The bottom part was made so you can just sweep the dirt into it."

Jaxon asks, "C-c-can I see it? Wait! We have one of those. Can I get it back so that I can c-c-clean up this mess?"

Dust Pan
Lloyd Ray

"Sure. Touch your necklace and say 'show me.'"

Jaxon does as he was told.

The dust pan pops into Mr. Ray's hand.

Jaxon jumps back startled. "N-n-no kidding! Is that h-h-how everything works? I mean, if I want you to b-b-bring something back, I just have to touch the necklace and say, 'sh-sh-show me.'" *I have to get a handle on this stuttering*, Jaxon thinks.

"In this particular case, yes, you can bring something back that way. But it depends on the situation—where you are, what it is, how big it is, and so on. Sometimes, we just bring stuff with us. You'll figure it out as you go along, son."

Mr. Ray smiles and hands Jaxon the dust pan. "See, it's great for cleaning up broken glass."

"But wait." Jaxon looks at the dustpan again, "Th-th-this is our dustpan. W-w-we have one just like the one you made a long time ago. That's really cool. Thanks for bringing it back."

"No problem. Glad to meet you, Jaxon," Mr. Ray utters softly.

"I think they use that k-k-kind of dust pan at the movie theater, too." Jaxon looks down and sees the broken glass and juice. "I'm g-g-gonna need the mop too," he says.

"Well, this guy here," Mr. Ray points to the other man, "is Thomas Stewart. He can help you with that. He created a mop that

Mop
Thomas Stewart

was better than the other kind they had—easier to use because he put something on it that could wring the mop without getting your hands wet."

"C-c-can I see it? Wait, oh yeah." He touches the necklace and says, "Show me."

The mop appears in Mr. Stewart's hand. "Take a look. As you can see, we wanted to make life's everyday chores a bit easier to do."

"You sure did!" Then Jaxon adds, "I d-d-don't mean to be rude, but wh-wh-why are you guys here?"

Mr. Stewart answers, "Because you said 'just imagine, what if there were no Black people in the world?' We are showing you what life might be like if there were no Black people around to invent things or make things better. And, son, this is just the beginning of your journey."

"J-j-journey? How long will it last?"

"Journey, adventure, call it what you like. It will last as long as you want it to."

"A-a-as long as I want? Really? That means I-I-I'm in charge. Awesome! I've never been the boss before. Okay, so how do I get my things back?"

"Your mom or sister can help you with that. They had the same necklace when they were girls and your grandmother did too."

"Whoa! Y-y-you knew my mom and my gr-gr-gran? Wait, and my s-s-sister, Raimy? They could see and talk to you too?"

"No, not us. They saw others," Mr. Ray replies. "Their wishes were different from yours. But they were just as curious as you are now. And they asked a lot of questions too, just like you're doing." He smiles broadly.

"Man! Th-th-that is so dope. Gran, Mom, and Raimy!" He's beaming. Thinking of his family reminds Jaxon to take a breath to calm down, which he does.

"I can't wait to talk to Raimy some more about this. I have so many questions."

Jaxon grabs the broom to start cleaning up his mess, then turns back to say something to Mr. Standard, but he's gone. Mr. Stewart and Mr. Ray, too. Poof! Just like that.

"Hey, Hey! Where'd you guys go?" Now he understands what Raimy meant about someone showing up.

So is this how it's going to be all day? Oh boy.

5
Magic in the Bathroom

KNOWING IT'S GOING to be a big day, Jaxon darts upstairs to get dressed. But first he has to wash his face and brush his hair, or his mom will have a fit. And with everything that's going on, he doesn't want to add his mom being mad at him.

Jaxon walks into the bathroom, opens the medicine cabinet on the wall next to the shower, and notices some things are missing. He doesn't see his hair brush or the oil for his hair. And there's an empty space where his mom's hot comb usually is.

"What the…Where's all the hair stuff?" He says out loud to no one, but just in case someone answers.

"Mornin', young man."

Madam C.J. Walker
Developed a Hair and Beauty Empire...

Jaxon nearly jumps out of his skin. Even though he was sorta expecting someone, it still startled him. He wonders if he's ever gonna get used to this.

"M-m-mornin," he says, moving backwards towards the door.

"My name is Madam C. J. Walker."

Hair Products
Madame C. J. Walker

He sees a tall pretty lady standing in front of him. She looks like someone very important, wearing dressy clothes and a hat with feathers and gloves.

"Those things are missing because I created hair products for Black folks' hair..."

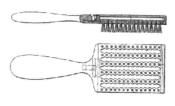

Brush
Lyda Newman

Another woman steps out from behind Madam Walker, "and I invented a new type of hair brush with bristles, making it easier to brush your thick bushy hair. My name is Lyda Newman."

"Whoa, y-y-you guys just p-p-pop in out of nowhere when I ask a question?"

"Well, yes," replies Miss Newman. "When the question has to do with a Black person inventing whatever it is you're asking about. We are all here in response to your 'just imagine' request."

He notices Miss Newman isn't as dressed up as Madame Walker, but she still looks nice in her white dress with lots of pink and yellow flowers on it. She's pretty too and has a nice smile.

"And your mom may have a bit of a problem getting her hair straight this morning because I invented the hot comb," adds a man with a big grin on his face.

Hot Comb
Walter Sammons

He's wearing a dark suit, with a tall hat on his head. He moves over to stand next to Madam Walker. "My name is Walter Sammons."

"Are y y-you kidding m-m-me?" *Stop stuttering. Stop stuttering. It's okay.* Jaxon takes a breath. He feels calmer and realizes how crowded the bathroom is. He shuffles back a couple steps.

"No, we're not kidding. There are plenty of other Black folks who created products for the hair, but we all couldn't fit into this bathroom," Madam Walker replies laughing.

They all laugh at that.

Jaxon remembers that in order to see the missing things, he has to say, 'show me.' So while they are still laughing, he touches his necklace and says, "Show me."

And then all three of them disappear right before his eyes. Poof! They're gone. He can't believe this is happening. Magic, again, right here, in his bathroom.

Jaxon looks over at the sink and sees that they left a black brush, an old-looking curling iron, and a couple of jars of hair stuff.

"Wow!" he shouts, shaking his head. "That was cool!"

Jaxon washes his face, brushes his hair and teeth, and hurries to his bedroom. His stuff is still gone.

6

Tennis Shoe Experiment

JAXON GETS HIS jeans and a blue t-shirt from the dresser and looks around for his tennis shoes.

"I know I put my tennis shoes under my bed. Okay, what did you do with my tennis shoes?" he asks crossing his arms. He's expecting someone this time.

"Maybe there wouldn't be any tennis shoes if it wasn't for me," states a young, good-looking man with wavy hair who materializes at the end of his bed.

"Folks wouldn't have been able to make a lot of shoes at the same time, if it wasn't for the machine I invented—the shoe lasting machine, that's what I called it. Made it possible to put the top of the shoe and the sole together quicker," he informs Jaxon.

"Who knows, making shoes by hand might've lasted forever, if it wasn't for me. My name is Jan Matzeliger."

Shoes
Jan Matzeliger

"M-m-Matzeliger?" Jaxon stops and takes a breath. "That's a funny name for a Black person. Where did you get that name?"

"From my father. He was Dutch and German, and my mother was from Africa," he explains.

"Well, I'm really glad you invented that shoe lasting machine Mr. Matzeliger because all I wear are tennis shoes. Mom makes me wear my dress shoes on Sunday when we go to church. But mostly I just wear tennis shoes. So thank you very much," he chuckles, wondering when he'll get his tennis shoes back and if it'll be any time soon.

"You're very welcome." Mr. Matzeliger stands up in front of Jaxon.

Jaxon looks up at him, "This is so awesome! I can't believe that saying, 'just imagine, what if there were no Black people in the world?' while wearing this necklace my gran gave me gives me the power to see and speak to you guys. I'm gonna put this all down in my journal."

He scans his room for his journal. He sees it and a pencil, but the pencil sharpener is missing.

"Did you happen to see a pencil sharpener anywhere in here?" he asks looking around the room.

Mr. Matzeliger points to the man standing behind Jaxon, "You might want to ask that guy behind you. I think he's responsible for the pencil sharpener."

Jaxon turns around. The man, now standing in front of him wearing a long, brown overcoat and brown boots, declares, "Yes, I am. My name is John Love. I made the portable pencil sharpener. I made it small enough so that you can carry it around with you in your backpack."

Jaxon takes another breath. "Well, thank goodness for that 'cause I break a lot of pencil leads. I like to keep a journal of exciting things that happen to me so that I can share with my class and my cousins."

Pencil Sharpener
John Love

"Well, today you'll have a lot of interesting things to write about," Mr. Love tells Jaxon, smiling. "I'm glad I could help. Keep up the good

school work. Word is you're doing very well in fourth grade." He winks.

"How do you know that?" Jaxon asks still mystified by it all.

"We know everything, Jaxon. We are with you all the time. We're your history, and history never goes away. And here's another piece of information—your laptop is missing because of

Dr. Mark Dean, a Black man who was instrumental in the invention of the personal computer."

"Yes, I was," Mr. Dean is standing next to Jaxon's bed, "along with the color monitor. I also figured out a way for your keyboard, mouse, printer, and laptop to communicate with each other."

"No way! That's awesome! Ah man, my Uncle Reggie should be here. He'd have a thousand questions for you. He's the computer genius in the family."

Personal Computer
Dr. Mark Dean

"That's good you have someone close who can help you navigate through computer problems when they come up. You're pretty good with the computer, too. I checked out some of what you have on your laptop."

"And like Mr. Love said, Jaxon," Mr. Dean continues, "you can't always see us, but we're always just a wish away." He bows and vanishes, just as Jaxon is saying, "show me."

Mr. Matzeliger disappears also, along with Mr. Love. Poof! Just like that!

Jaxon sits down on his bed and thinks about what Mr. Dean told him. So many crazy thoughts are running around his brain. *I'm only 9 years old. Am I special?*

He's holding his head down and sees his tennis shoes next to his feet. He looks up and sees his laptop and pencil sharpener are back on his desk.

"For real?" he says out loud.

Then he gets a brilliant idea.

What if I wish for all the styles and colors of MJ sneakers? Can't be that many, could it? Yeah, Raimy said to be careful what I ask for, but what harm would it be to wish for tennis shoes?

Jaxon really, really wants a pair, but his mom refuses to pay over $100 for tennis shoes. So he decides to make another wish. He says, "Just imagine, I have all the MJ sneakers and colors in my size, in my bedroom, right now."

All of a sudden, it's pitch black in his room, and he can hardly breathe. The smell of new rubber shoes is overpowering. He's lying on his stomach, face down, on the floor with a ton of tennis shoes on top of him. He turns his head a bit, but he can't see anything. He tries not to panic, but he's scared. He doesn't like the dark. He starts to feel a little dizzy.

Jaxon calls out to his mom, but she doesn't come. Then he whispers loudly, "Gran, Gran, please help me. I'm scared Gran, please help me."

He tries to figure out where he is in his bedroom. He has a horrible time turning around. Every time he moves shoes shift and fall on him. He continues to wiggle trying to move himself forward. He lays there for what seems like forever trying to figure out what to do next. He fights the dizzy scared feeling. He tries pushing his body forward and then, all of a sudden, he's able to move a little bit. Then he sees some light in front of him. It may be the light from the hallway, but he's not sure. He's still having a hard time breathing. He'd better think of something fast.

He decides to try using his arms to pull himself in the direction of the light, hoping it's the hallway. Slowly and carefully, he starts pulling himself towards the light. Getting closer, he sees the light is actually to his right, so he turns sharply and shoes fall in front of him. He continues to move slowly and the shoes move out of his way slightly. It takes what seems like forever, but finally he's almost at the doorway. The light is getting brighter, and he can see the bottom of the linen closet door in front of his bedroom.

Jaxon finally gets himself where he can crawl out into the hallway. He turns over on his back and starts breathing the fresh air. He whispers, "Thanks Gran. I know it was you who helped me outta there."

He sits up on the floor and looks at his bedroom. It's packed to the ceiling with tennis shoes—black, red, blue, green, high top, low top, leather, suede, Velcro, shoelaces. He can't believe his eyes.

"Michael Jordan, you sure make a lot of shoes." And then, he realizes he could have run out of air and gotten trapped in there or been smashed to death. He wonders, *How long was I under there? Hours? Nah…but it sure seemed like it.*

He stands up, brushes himself off, and says, "Thanks again, Gran." Then he heads downstairs.

Halfway down the stairs, he looks back into his room and realizes, *I need to figure out how to get rid of those shoes before my mom sees them.* He has no idea what to do about the tennis shoes.

He scrambles back up the stairs and closes his bedroom door. At least she won't see them if she walks by. *I'll figure out the rest later. Maybe one of these smart inventors will know.*

Jaxon believes, with all his heart, that he escaped those sneakers because of his gran. There is no other explanation. He shudders thinking about what could have happened and how truly bad it could have turned out. Raimy really meant business when she told him not to wish for anything crazy that could hurt someone. Like him.

7

Gran's Phone

JAXON HEADS BACK downstairs in a flash, anxious to see who else is visiting him today.

He scans the living room again and notices his grandmother's old telephone is still gone. His mom told him she kept Gran's phone to remind her how much the phone has changed over the years.

Jaxon remembers when he first saw the telephone, a few years ago. His mom brought it up from the basement. He had no clue what it was. It was so clunky-looking and had a dial with numbers on it. It was hard to believe they used to use it instead of a cell phone. He couldn't figure out how it worked until his mother used it to call his father at work one day.

He takes a good breath to calm himself and says aloud, "Where's Gran's phone?" expecting someone to show up. And sure enough, someone does.

"Well, that's a long story," answers a thin, dark man standing in the middle of the living room. "But I'll keep it short and sweet. You see, Alexander Graham Bell, the inventor of the telephone, actually used some of my technology for his telephone. Do you know what a telegraph is?"

"N-n-no, I never heard of it," replies Jaxon, taking another deep breath to calm himself while he waits for the explanation he's pretty sure is coming.

"A telegraph was a machine that allowed people to communicate over long distances using something called Morse code. Short and long sounds were used to represent letters. Well, what I invented

was actually a telegraph transmitter which combined the telephone and telegraph."

"Wow! Really? That's awesome."

"My name is Granville Woods, and in some books they don't even mention me. The same with other things I invented. I didn't get credit for them either." He shakes his head, with a somber look on his face.

"But, why? That's not fair."

GRANVILLE T. WOODS.

Granville Woods

"No it wasn't, but it's the way things were back then, son. I invented a lot of things. Mostly things to do with trains communicating with each other to make sure they traveled through the cities safely," he explains, lifting his head with pride and smiling.

"Awesome! You must be extra smart!" Jaxon studies Mr. Woods. *He's pretty tall too.*

"Jaxon, I studied hard and read a lot. You can be just as smart, as long as you stay in school and read as much as you can. Stay curious, Jaxon. Curiosity will be the key to you wanting to learn even more." Mr. Woods nods as if agreeing with himself.

"College is a good idea too."

"My mom and dad tell me that all the time. And speaking of curiosity, I have a question. Who decides which inventions and inventors I see? And can you show me Gran's phone, please?"

The phone doesn't show up.

He remembers he's supposed to touch the necklace and say "show me." He moves his hand to his neck and just feels his neck. The necklace is not there!

"Oh no! Wh-wh-where's my necklace? I j-j-just had it a minute ago before I came downstairs. I didn't t-t-take it off. I never take it off."

"Just think for a minute, Jaxon. It has to be here somewhere. Do you remember when you used it last?" Mr. Woods asks.

"I-I-I think in my bedroom," Jaxon says.

What if I don't find the necklace?

"Why don't you go back upstairs real quick and see if it fell on the floor. Or maybe you kicked it under the furniture if it fell off. It can't be far, Jaxon, if you just had it."

Jaxon blasts up the stairs. He stops at the top and looks at the bathroom. He thinks, *It could have fallen off in there. This is so weird, it's never fallen off before. How could this happen?*

He walks into the bathroom and looks in the shower, in all the drawers. No necklace. He opens the medicine cabinet. Not there. He checks the cabinets under the sink. Not there either. Looks under the rugs. The necklace is nowhere to be seen.

He hurries over to his bedroom and opens his door. The piles and piles of tennis shoes are still there. How can he look for it in his bedroom? He scans the shoes in the front of the pile and doesn't see the necklace. He really starts to sweat now. *What about my wishes? Oh no! How will I get things back the way they were? What will I tell Mom?*

He just stands there, on the verge of tears, then gets down on his hands and knees and starts pulling shoes away from the pile, breathing hard. When he pulls out a black sneaker, he sees something shiny in the blue sneaker behind it. Could it be the necklace chain?

He scoots a little closer and pulls the necklace from the blue sneaker under the pile. It must have gotten pulled off him when he was scooting around the pile of shoes and he was too scared to notice. He holds the necklace tight and smiles broadly.

Looking up, Jaxon whispers, "Thanks Gran. You saved me again."

He puts the necklace back on and pats it under his shirt to make sure it's there, then bolts back downstairs. He stands in front of Mr. Woods, showing him the necklace.

"Well that's a relief, for sure," says Mr. Woods grinning.

"Yes and s-s-sorry for running off like that." Jaxon takes a breath to calm himself.

He touches the necklace and says, "Please show me Gran's phone."

The phone appears on the table where it usually sits.

Mr. Woods looks at the phone and then back at Jaxon, "To answer your question about who decides which inventions and inventors you see—depends on where you are, what you ask for, and what you're doing at the time. It would be impossible to show you everything Black people invented all at once. So we just show you a few things at a time. We try to select inventions and discoveries that you will understand. And as you get older, if you make the same wish, the inventions may become more complex.

"It's also good for you to meet folks from a long time ago, like the 1800s and 1900s. We think it's important for you to see that Black people have always been intelligent, creative, aware, nurturing, and very proud. Life was very different and difficult for Black folks back then. But we had a lot of drive, and still we kept moving forward.

"Listen Jaxon, as you use your magic, you can continue to learn more about your history and the effect Black American inventors and scientists have had on our society.

"I hope I answered your questions. Sorry I can't stay any longer. The magic only allows us to stay around for a few minutes. Have to go. Have a great day!" Mr. Woods vanishes. Poof! He's gone.

Jaxon stands there and stares at the empty spot when, *whoa*, right before his very eyes Dr. Martin Luther King, Jr. himself appears right here, in his house, in his living room.

8

Meeting the King

JAXON ALMOST FALLS backwards on the floor. His mouth drops open.

"D-D-Dr. Martin Luther K-K-King!" he says a bit louder than he means to. "Wh-wh-what are you doing here? D-d-did I wish for you too?" He gazes at the man whose face he's seen in so many books, on television, and in pictures in stores and people's homes.

Dr. Martin Luther King

"Hello, Jaxon," a deep, familiar voice replies. "I understand you're playing me in your school play next week. And you're working very hard in rehearsal. I am honored," Dr. King says smiling.

Jaxon's hands are shaking, and his knees are too, a little bit. "Th-th-thanks," he says. He takes a deep breath to try to calm himself, but it's Martin Luther King!

"I can't begin to tell you how important your experience today and the experiences you may have later, with other inventors and scientists, are going to be for you, your family, and your friends." Dr. King is looking straight at Jaxon. "Used correctly, you can learn a great amount of history from that necklace."

"N-n-no offense Dr. King, but wh-wh-why are you here?" Jaxon takes another breath. "Everyone I've seen so far has been an inventor. Did you invent something?"

"Well, no. I'm here because you mentioned me earlier. Those of us who are considered historical figures appear when the magic words relate to Black history. As far as I know, this type of wish has only come up once before in your family. It was your Great-great-great-great Aunt Anna. The short version of the story is that she was fussing one day about all the chores she had to do in what they called "the big house." And in her upset state she blurted out, "Just imagine, what if there were no colored folks? What would they do then?"

"After she spoke those words, all the Black folks other than her disappeared in the house and in the fields. Everybody. Scared her to death. When I think back on how the story was told to me, everybody else in the house went wild. Food was left cooking on the stove, clothes were lying on the floors, and tools were lying in the fields.

"Anna ran out the back door so no one could see her and ask her what happened. At first, she didn't know what to make of it. Then she realized she'd said the magic words. As far as I know it was only the second time she had used the necklace to make a wish, even though she really didn't mean to make that wish.

"The way the story goes is that she went out back to the barn and hid in the stable behind a horse. When she finally came to terms with what she had done, she decided to let the slave owners see how valuable Black folks were to them. And even though she couldn't see what was happening, she knew there was a great amount of confusion going on.

"The next morning her father found her asleep in the stable. He woke her and told her to put everything back. She was startled at first seeing her father. But then she remembered that he knew about her and the magic, and that the magic didn't affect him.

"He hadn't been on the farm when she made the wish. He had gone to town to get supplies, and it was late when he returned. He knew that something had happened because as he was driving the wagon back to the farm, he didn't see any Black people anywhere. He decided to bed down in the wagon and look into what happened the next morning.

"In the morning when it was light, he drove to the back of the barn, which he knew was Anna's favorite hiding place, and found her there.

"Her father told her that she had had her fun for a day, but it was time to undo her wish. She resisted a little, but she knew he was right. She just hoped the slave owners would remember how valuable the work of Black people was to them.

"So Jaxon, as far as I know, you are one of very few people who has made a wish about no Black people."

"That's a really cool story. And if she hadn't put things back, we wouldn't be here."

"You could be right," Dr. King responds looking as if he's thinking about something.

"I am also here to inform you that if you take someone on a magical venture with you, like the one you're on today, when you undo your wish, they will not remember meeting any of the inventors or scientists. But they will remember their history." He smiles.

Then his smile gets bigger, "So next month, when your cousin Kevin comes to visit, you might want to remember what I'm telling you."

Jaxon feels his eyes get a little tickly. "Wow, D-d-dr. King you helped make m-m-my world a better place, and n-n-now..." Jaxon stopped and took a breath. "Now you're helping me with my new magic. I want to do a great job being you in the play, but I-I-I'm afraid my stuttering will get in the way of your great words."

"Jaxon, don't worry about the play, you're going to do just fine." Dr. King pauses for a moment and looks up. Then he looks right at Jaxon and says, "This reminds me of something I once said. Please remember this: 'Be a bush if you can't be a tree. If you can't be a highway, just be a trail. If you can't be a sun, be a star. For it isn't by size that you win or fail. Be the best of whatever you are.'"

After that, Dr. King disappears right before Jaxon's eyes. Poof! He vanishes.

"Wait! Don't go yet!" Jaxon calls out. He is not ready for Dr. King to leave. He has so many questions. And how is being a bush or a trail going to help him in the play?

Jaxon just stands there, in the middle of the living room, gazing at the space where Dr. King had been standing. Then he steps into the space where Dr. King was, hoping to feel something. He doesn't know what. Just something.

9

Magic in the Front Yard

JAXON IS STILL stunned that Dr. King was in his house a minute ago. He was actually talking to him.

He wishes he could tell someone, and then he spots Gran's old phone sitting on the table. He decides to call his dad to tell him about his day and to make sure he'll still be home around noon. He picks up the part of the phone you put by your ear and talk into and laughs to himself because he actually remembers how to use it. He reaches down to the other part on the table and dials the number to his dad's office.

When his dad answers, Jaxon starts talking very fast.

"Hey Dad, sorry to bother you at work. But it's really been an awesome morning. I found out the necklace Gran gave me is magic! And I've been meeting and talking to Black people from history, Dad!"

"Jaxon, are you okay?"

"Yeah Dad, I've never been better."

"I'm sorry son, but I have to get to a meeting, like now. We'll talk more when I get home. I promise I'll be home by noon." Jaxon hears the click of his dad hanging up.

Jaxon, sad, drops his head down even though he's used to his dad and his meetings. He knows his dad will remember to talk to him about their phone call when he gets home. But he really wanted to tell him now.

Jaxon is just standing there with no idea what to do next thinking, *So now what? Oh, right!* He remembers that he didn't get the paper off the porch like he usually does every morning. He walks to the door, opens it, and freaks out. He throws his hands in the air with his mouth wide open because the lawn looks like a miniature jungle even though he just mowed it yesterday.

Then he realizes he's probably about to meet somebody responsible for this. He takes a breath and looks around. Sure enough, there's a man sitting on the porch, eating an apple.

"Hello," Jaxon utters as he strolls towards him.

"Hello, Jaxon. Looks like you have a big job ahead of you."

"Yeah, especially since I just mowed the lawn yesterday," he replies with a frown.

"Well, sorry about that. It'll still be a pretty easy job because I designed a lawn mower that's easy to push through the grass. My name is John Burr, by the way," offering his hand for Jaxon to shake.

Jaxon gets closer, shakes Mr. Burr's hand, and laughs, "Nice to meet you sir, but I *did* mow the lawn yesterday!"

"Yes you did. And you *did* say the magic words, 'just imagine.' So as a result, what you see is what you get."

Jaxon thinks, *Okay, so with you, I get grass up to my knees and have to mow the lawn again*. He says, "This would

Lawn Mower
John Burr

sure be a lot of work without a lawnmower."

"Indeed, it would." Mr. Burr stands up and throws the apple to Jaxon.

"Have a wonderful day, Jaxon."

Jaxon catches the apple, and Mr. Burr disappears. Poof! Just like that.

But the apple doesn't disappear. It changes. Jaxon wonders how and why it's a fresh, new apple and not the one Mr. Burr was eating.

Now that's a cool trick, he thinks.

But, right now, the why and the how aren't very important because it's a bright red, juicy apple, and Jaxon is hungry. He decides to see if it tastes as good as it looks. He takes a big bite, and as it turns out, it's delicious.

Jaxon picks up the paper and then remembers the lawn. He pulls out the necklace and says, "Show me." A lawnmower appears by the

fence. He turns to look at the lawn again. It looks freshly cut just like it did yesterday! *Now that's an even cooler trick*, he thinks.

He smiles and goes back into the house, eating the delicious apple delivered to him from the past.

10

Dad Comes Home

JAXON PUTS THE newspaper on the kitchen table for his mom. He wonders where she is. He hopes she isn't in his room. He races up the stairs to make sure his bedroom door is still closed. He hasn't figured out how to make the shoes go away, yet. He can't use his last wish. Looking at the closed door, he thinks, *I really don't want to have the sneaker discussion with Mom.*

He heads back downstairs to the kitchen, finishes the apple, and tosses the core in the trash can. He looks at the clock and thinks, *Where has the morning gone?* But after giving it some thought, he realizes a lot has happened this morning.

He's still hungry, so he decides to have that bowl of cereal and glass of orange juice he didn't get to eat and drink earlier. He sits down at the table to eat, picks up the paper, and reads the comics.

After a little while, he cleans his dishes and walks into the living room. Then he hears the front door open. It's his dad.

That's right. It is close to noon.

His dad has a peculiar look on his face. He seems to be in a daze.

"What's wrong, Dad? Are you okay?"

Jaxon hears something and turns to see his mom scurrying down the stairs. She looks at his dad and asks worriedly, "Joe, are you okay? You look like you've seen a ghost."

Jaxon watches his mom come down the stairs. He's thinking, *Wow, Mom just shows up and Dad's home early.*

"Not a ghost. But something is just not right."

Jaxon looks at his mom. She winks at him and smiles.

Jaxon is a little confused about the wink. Then he decides his mom must know about him and the necklace.

"Tell us what happened," she says.

His dad shakes his head and begins to talk. "It started right after I spoke with Jaxon earlier today. I hung up the phone and walked out of the office to the elevator to go to my meeting. The elevator wasn't there. It took me a minute to realize it really wasn't there. I just stood there staring at a blank wall."

"So I walked up ten floors of stairs," he says frowning, "Not fun."

"Sorry about that," a man sitting on the sofa with a big mustache responds. "My name is Alexander Miles, and the elevator was not there because I created the design for an automatic opening and closing elevator door."

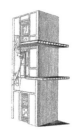

Elevator
Alexander Miles

Jaxon's father looks at the man, shocked. He walks toward him firing questions, "Who the heck are you? How did you get in here?"

Jaxon runs and puts his hand on his dad's arm, "Dad, I can explain."

As quickly as he can, Jaxon tells his dad about the necklace, Gran, his wish, and what's been happening today.

Jaxon's mom reminds his dad about Raimy and her experiences with the necklace.

"Raimy told me this morning that she and Jaxon had a talk about the necklace last night. I was going to talk to him first thing, but I had to run next door to Mrs. Moore's house to give her a hand with the back door. You know how it sticks sometimes, and she can't get it open. And of course, she found other things she needed done. I was over there much longer than I planned to be. So I didn't get a chance before now to talk to Jaxon.

"That's what Jaxon was trying to tell me about earlier, and I had to hang up to go to my meeting. Sorry," his dad murmurs, still giving the man a suspicious look.

Jaxon's father seems to have calmed down a bit. "I suppose that explains the other things I experienced today. Like, after I left the building, I walked to the corner where I usually drop the mail, and the mailbox wasn't there."

"That would be because of me," says a man sitting in the exact same spot where Mr. Miles had been sitting. No one noticed that Mr. Miles had vanished.

"Hold up! Where's the other guy?" his dad asks truly freaked out now. "Who are you?"

"My name is Philip Downing. I invented a mailbox that was more secure than the old one. I created an inner safety door which protects the mail from thieves and bad weather conditions," he shares proudly.

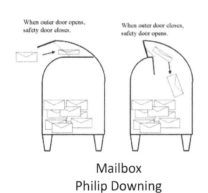

When outer door opens, safety door closes.

When outer door closes, safety door opens.

Mailbox
Philip Downing

Jaxon's dad just stands there looking at the guy. And then, appearing to be okay with what he's hearing, he says, "No kidding." He walks over to Mr. Downing and shakes his hand. "That's impressive and sad."

"Sad? Why Dad?"

"Because I was not taught, your mom was not taught, your sister was not taught, and you aren't being taught about the many inventions Black people have provided this country. While I am happy we're learning these things now, I feel sad and angry that we didn't know before."

Jaxon is not sure what to think about his dad's reaction.

His dad continues, "It's cool you can talk to people about their inventions. And meeting them is even more amazing. It's really exciting for me, that's for sure."

All of a sudden, Jaxon's dad looks like he's remembering something.

"You know, it just dawned on me. After I spoke with you, I didn't see any Black people in my office or on my way home. That was the other thing that was really strange to me. It makes sense now."

Wait, not just Black people's inventions are missing, but Black people too. Jaxon's stomach feels sick.

"Jaxon, come with me to the study. I have a book I'd like you to see."

Jaxon decides to think about the scary thought later. He will have to be very careful with his last wish.

His dad turns to thank Mr. Downing for providing his information, but Mr. Downing is gone.

He flashes a questioning look at Jaxon. Jaxon puts his hand on his dad's back and says, "Don't worry, you'll get used to it. Huh, Mom?"

She looks at Jaxon's dad amused, "Yes, Joe, we are part of his extraordinary day, too."

11

Magic in the Study

JAXON FOLLOWS HIS dad into the study. It has a ton of books, a big desk, and a puffy leather chair. His dad spends a lot of time in here reading.

His dad is staring at the desk. "What happened to the lamp?"

"Hello there," says a good-looking man wearing big black rimmed glasses, standing next to the bookcase. "The lamp is not there because of me."

Jaxon asks, "Did you invent the lamp?"

"No, I invented a small thing inside the light bulb that keeps it lit for a long time."

Light Bulb Filament
Lewis Latimer

"Really!" Jaxon and his dad blurt out at the same time. Then they look at each other and smile.

"Yes, my name is Lewis Latimer," the man continues. "You see, Thomas Edison invented the light bulb, but his bulb would only stay on for a very short period of time. With the filament I invented, the bulb will stay on for hours and hours."

"You're kidding!" Jaxon's dad is truly impressed.

"No, I actually did."

Jaxon touches his necklace and says, "Show me." The lamp appears on the desk. Jaxon walks over to the desk and turns it on.

"Whoa!" says Jaxon's dad. "That's quite a trick. And what's with the 'show me'?"

"When the inventors show up, in order for me to see their inventions I have to touch my necklace and say, 'show me.'"

"Cool. Oh, sorry for the interruption," Jaxon's dad says turning back to Mr. Latimer.

"No problem. I also worked for Alexander Graham Bell. I helped him write his patent for the telephone. Jaxon, that means that I helped him write the document to send to the government to make it illegal for anyone to steal his invention." Mr. Latimer smiles proudly.

Jaxon's truly impressed. "Wow! That's awesome! And I learned earlier that Mr. Granville Woods also helped Mr. Bell with the telephone. So two Black people helped Mr. Bell's telephone invention. How cool is that!"

Then Jaxon feels a little sad. "We learned about Mr. Bell in class. But they didn't mention you or Mr. Woods."

"Yes, I know. Maybe one day this will change, and we'll be included in the history books."

"Let's hope," says Jaxon's dad. "I can't believe you don't get credit in the history books."

"That's the way things have been. Now you two know about me. What will it take for more people to know about Black inventors and scientists?"

And with that, Mr. Latimer disappears. Poof! Just like that.

The question sits with Jaxon, *What will it take for people to know?*

His dad shakes his head and continues talking. "Jaxon, I have something I want to share with you. I was in my Black Studies class in college when my grandmother had a heart attack. When I told my professor why I had to take a few days off, he gave me a gift—a book to read while I was away."

Jaxon's dad grabs a book off the shelf. "I've kept it all this time. It's a book about a couple of famous African American doctors."

"Famous African American doctors? What are their names?"

His dad opens the book and finds the names. "Come here, do you recognize either of these names?"

"Dr. Charles Drew and Dr. Daniel Hale Williams," Jaxon reads aloud. "I think I heard of Dr. Drew."

"Well, thank you very much for inviting us in," states a gentleman in a white coat with a stethoscope hanging around his neck. He is standing near the doorway with another man in a white coat who has a bushy mustache.

"My name is Dr. Drew," says the man with the stethoscope.

"I'm Dr. Williams," says the man with the bushy mustache.

Blood Bank
Dr. Charles Drew

Dr. Daniel Hale Williams

"Really!" Jaxon's dad walks over to the doctors, extending his hand to both men and smiling broadly. "This is a real pleasure."

"The pleasure is ours as well."

Dr. Williams looks at Jaxon. "Dr. Drew created the first blood bank. Have you ever heard of a blood bank?"

"Yes, I learned about it during Health Day at school. It's a place where people donate blood, and if you get sick and don't have enough of your own, you can get some from the blood bank."

"Correct," Dr. Drew responds.

"Jaxon, I was the first doctor to perform open heart surgery," Dr. Williams shares.

"Wow," is all Jaxon could say, thinking about this man being the very first to perform that important surgery.

And then it dawns on him. "Wait a minute. If you hadn't performed the first heart surgery, maybe my dad's grandmother would have died when she had the heart attack."

Then he turns and looks at his dad. "She was okay after the surgery, right?"

"Yes, the surgery was successful. She lived many years after that, thanks to Dr. Williams."

Dr. Drew turns to Jaxon's dad. "Thank you for introducing us. We don't get talked about very much. It is our hope that our stories will inspire young people to get into medicine." He looks directly at Jaxon and winks.

Jaxon walks over and stands in front of Dr. Drew, and he looks up at him admiringly. "This has been the best day of my life, meeting and talking to all of you. I feel like, I don't know, I'm in dreamland or something. I can't wait to share what I'm learning with my cousins, Kevin and Madison, and with my class."

"That would be great. Maybe one of them will think about getting into medicine, too," Dr. Williams says smiling.

Then, the fine doctors disappear. Poof! Just like that.

Jaxon's dad looks at Jaxon with a disturbed expression on his face. "Do you ever get used to that?"

12

The Third Wish

JAXON TURNS AND sees his mom standing in the study doorway. She's probably been standing there the whole time. She has a serious look on her face.

"Joe, I need to let you know what happens to people when Jaxon puts everything back the way it was. People who have not had the necklace, like Raimy and I have, will not remember what happened to them. So you won't remember talking to Dr. Drew and Dr. Williams, or to Mr. Latimer."

Some of the excitement leaves Jaxon's dad's face.

"Are you serious? I won't remember any of the conversations? That, somehow, seems unfair," he says frowning.

"Listen honey, Jaxon doesn't have any control over what happens when things go back the way they were. It's just the way it is. I'm sorry."

"At least Jaxon will remember, and that's cool," his dad says.

Jaxon smiles remembering something. "Dad, Dr. King told me that even though you won't remember the people, you will remember what you learned about them."

"That helps," his dad says, "but...did you just say..."

His mom interrupts. "Whoa! Did you just say you met Dr. King...like Dr. Martin Luther King, Junior?"

"Yeah, it was awesome. He's even better in person."

"That's really something," says his mom, smiling and shaking her head.

Jaxon feels his own huge smile. "He even said something to

help me with the play. It was something about if you can't be a tree be a bush, if you can't be a highway be a trail..."

"I know that quote!" says Jaxon's dad, "It ends with, 'Be the best of whatever you are.'"

"That's right!" Jaxon says beaming. "Now I think I get it. I'm not going to be him, but I'm going to be the best me playing him. And did you notice I wasn't stuttering when I was talking to Mr. Latimer and the two doctors? I was stuttering a whole lot when I first met the scientists and inventors. Oh man! I practiced remembering my breathing all morning. And the more I talked to them, the easier it got.

"Even if I stutter a little during the play, I know my lines and I know how to calm down—I'll still be the best that I can. That means I'm gonna nail that play about the great Dr. King!"

"Good for you, son!" says his dad.

"That's terrific, Jaxon! We know you'll do a great job," says his mom.

Jaxon gets serious. "It's been a super morning, but it really bothers me that Black people are missing because of my wish. And I'm ready to play ball with Dad. So Mom, how *do* I put everything back the way it was?"

"You say, 'just imagine, I undo my wish' and things will go back to how they would be if you hadn't made the wish. If you made two wishes in the month, you would say 'I undo my wishes.' If you want to undo just one of the wishes or a wish from another month, you'd have to specify the wish. Make sense?"

Jaxon nods.

"Remember, you only have three wishes a month. Changing things back counts as a wish too. Our family learned a long time ago that you should always save one wish, just in case. So really you only get two wishes. Keep that in mind."

"Yes, Ma'am."

"And Jaxon, I know Raimy told you this too, but don't go messin' around and asking for something crazy."

"Okay, Mom," says Jaxon, "I won't."

"Time to put things back the way they were," Jaxon announces.

"Okay. And don't be surprised if you end up in a different room or a different place in the house or even in a different time of day."

Jaxon looks a little worried.

"But it will all seem natural to you when it happens. You'll see," his mom assures him, patting him on the shoulder.

Jaxon relaxes and can't wait to see what happens when things get back to normal—and finally get rid of those shoes.

"Okay wait! I have a question. How come you, dad, Raimy, and me are still here? I said 'no Black people.' Are we special or something?"

"Good question. I don't have a real answer for that, other than you will always be able to see me, your dad, and Raimy. I remember Gran saying something about immediate family automatically gets pulled into your wish—no matter where they are, like what happened with Dad today, for instance.

"I didn't make the kind of wish you made, so I'm not really sure. But if anyone else is present when you make your wish, they will participate in the wish. They just won't remember afterwards, like Dad won't. I don't really know why, Jaxon. You understand?"

"Yep. Got it. Okay, here we go." He removes the necklace from under his shirt, holds the little blue pendant in his hand and says, "Just imagine, I undo my wishes."

He sees his mom's eyebrows go up a little when he says "wishes," but the next thing he knows, he and his dad are in the living room getting ready to head out the door to play ball.

Jaxon looks around and everything seems to be back to normal.

He pokes his head in the kitchen. Their refrigerator is back, along with the dustpan and mop. And the floor is clean.

When he comes out of the kitchen, Jaxon sees his dad has gone into the study and is turning off the lamp.

"Don't forget your baseball glove and bat," his dad reminds him.

"Yep," says Jaxon. He pauses, then says, "You know...a Black man named Lewis Latimer invented something that makes the light bulb stay on." He watches his dad carefully.

His dad looks up at the ceiling and then back at Jaxon and says, "Yeah. Yeah, I know that. Hmmm, I don't remember how. But that's cool. Okay, get your gear and I'll meet you in the car."

Jaxon rushes upstairs to his room to get his gear. He is relieved to see that his stuff is back and even better, the sneakers are gone. *Thank goodness!*

He checks the bathroom, and the hair stuff is back in place. He sprints back down the stairs two at a time.

"See you guys later," his mom yells from the top of the stairs. She winks at Jaxon and waves.

"See you later, Mom." He grins and waves back.

"I'm coming, Dad. I have my glove and bat!"

As Jaxon closes the door, he thinks, *What a cool day this has been. Can't imagine how I'll top this next time.*

Acknowledgments

I can't imagine anyone taking on a project like this, specifically writing a book, without the help of a village. I'll start with my husband Ernest who just nods and asks, "How much?" Thanks, honey.

Then my daughter Tanisha, who's been after me to rewrite these books forever. So thanks for the push, sweetie.

Suze Allen, my writing coach, helped me get this puppy off the ground. She saw my vision and we took off.

I can't say enough about Karin Fisher-Golton, my editor. She has that kid thing going on. I'm really, really grateful for her patience, and she too saw my vision.

Thanks to Jo Ann Kairys, my graphic artist, who put life into the book. We decided to do something different, and it just works. What a visionary.

Thanks to Monica Thomas who designed a great cover.

And then there's Nick. So let's get back to patience. Without going into that little adventure, let's just say I'm glad he's still talking to me. A great guy. Thanks, Nick.

And then there's my family and friends who probably are happy the first book is out, and we can start talking about something else and book two. Thank you all for being there for me. Yes, I have a village and I am grateful to all of them.

Also available for purchase are Jaxon's Journal, Jaxon's Activity Book and Jaxon's Coloring Book!

Did you have fun reading about Jaxon's experience meeting African American inventors and scientists?

Well, stay tuned, because there are more books coming in 2018!

Book Two   Jaxon and Kevin's Black History Adventure Downtown

Book Three Let's Hear It for the Girl Inventors and Scientists!

Book Four   Jaxon's Visit at NASA

Book Five   Jaxon Meets Deadwood Dick

About the Author

Tamara Shiloh is on a mission to help children learn about Black history and those other hidden figures in American history. She is doing this with her children's book series, *Just Imagine…What If There Were No Black People in the World?*—a series about African American inventors and scientists. Her first book in the series, *Jaxon's Magical Adventure with Black Inventors and Scientists* is accompanied by a journal, activity book with puzzles, and coloring book. Her goal is to engage children by providing a fun and magical book with informative information that hopefully inspires children to want to participate in STEM programs and pursue STEM careers. She speaks on the importance of teaching Black history all year to all children.

Tamara believes that teaching Black history to young children will maintain good relationships, improve relationships, provide mentors and build good self-esteem for Black children. She lives in Northern California.

You can visit her website at **www.tamarashiloh.com** to learn more about her and her children's books series.

Copy this form or Order Online

WWW.TAMARASHILOH.COM

Order Form

Date: _____

Ordered by:
Name: _____

Address: _____

_____

Email: _____

Ship to: (if different):
Name: _____

Address: _____

Email: _____

Qty	Description	Print Price	Shipping	Total
	Book (Paperback)	$8.99	$3.00 each	
	Jaxon's Journal	$6.99	$2.50 each	
	Jaxon's Workbook	$5.99	$3.50 each	
	Jaxon's Coloring Box	$4.99	$2.90 each	
	Book (eBook)	$2.99	N/A	
	SET	$23.00	$4.00 set	
	Thank you for your business!		Sub-total	
			Discount	
			Shipping	
			Sales Tax	
	Checks payable to: *Just Imagine Books & Services*		TOTAL	

Credit Card: #_____

Exp: _____/_____   CVC: _____   Zip Code: _____

Signature: _____

Just Imagine Books & Services
102 Washington Ave, Suite 8, Richmond, CA 94801 // 510-422-5304
www.tamarashiloh.com // admin@tamarashiloh.com

CPSIA information can be obtained
at www.ICGtesting.com
Printed in the USA
FSHW01n1555231018
53179FS